Every Time I Climb a Tree

and Other Poems

Contents

Every Time I Climb a Tree

Every time I climb a tree
Every time I climb a tree
Every time I climb a tree
I scrape a leg
Or skin a knee
And every time I climb a tree
I find some ants
Or dodge a bee
And get the ants
All over me.

And every time I climb a tree
Where have you been?
They say to me
But don't they know that I am free
Every time I climb a tree?

I like it best
To spot a nest
That has an egg
Or maybe three.

And then I skin
The other leg
But every time I climb a tree
I see a lot of things to see
Swallows rooftops and TV
And all the fields and farms there be
Every time I climb a tree
Though climbing may be good for ants
It isn't awfully good for pants
But still it's pretty good for me
Every time I climb a tree.

David McCord

Ode to My Shoes

my shoes
rest
all night
under my bed

tired
they stretch
and loosen
their laces

wide open
they fall asleep
and dream
of walking

they revisit
the places
they went to
during the day

and wake up
cheerful
relaxed
so soft

Francisco X. Alarcón

Cats

Cats sleep, anywhere,
Any table, any chair
Top of piano, window-ledge,
In the middle, on the edge,
Open drawer, empty shoe,
Anybody's lap will do,
Fitted in a cardboard box,
In the cupboard, with your frocks.
Anywhere! They don't care–
Cats sleep anywhere.

Eleanor Farjeon

Porcupines

Hugging you takes some practice.
So I'll start out with a cactus.

Marilyn Singer

A Doctor from Near Aberdeen

A doctor from near Aberdeen
Had a pet anaconda called Jean
If you said, 'Please',
She'd give you a squeeze,
But few of the patients were keen.

Michael Palin

Who Has Seen the Wind?

Who has seen the wind?
Neither I nor you:
But when the leaves hang trembling,
The wind is passing through.

Who has seen the wind?
Neither you nor I:
But when the trees bow down their heads,
The wind is passing by.

Christina Rossetti

The Schoolkids' Rap

Miss was at the blackboard writing with the chalk,
When suddenly she stopped in the middle of her talk.
She snapped her fingers – snap! snap! snap!
Pay attention, children, and I'll teach you how to rap.

She picked up a pencil, she started to tap.
All together, children, now, clap! clap! clap!
Just get the rhythm, just get the beat.
Drum it with your fingers, stamp it with your feet.

That's right, children, keep in time.
Now we've got the rhythm, all we need is the rhyme.
This school is cool, Miss Grace is ace.
Strut your stuff with a smile on your face.

Snap those fingers, tap those toes.
Do it like they do on the video shows.
Flap it! Slap it! Clap! Snap! Clap!
Let's all do the schoolkids' rap!

John Foster

Be Glad Your Nose Is on Your Face

Be glad your nose is on your face,
not pasted on some other place,
for if it were where it is not,
you might dislike your nose a lot.

Imagine if your precious nose
were sandwiched in between your toes,
that clearly would not be a treat,
for you'd be forced to smell your feet.

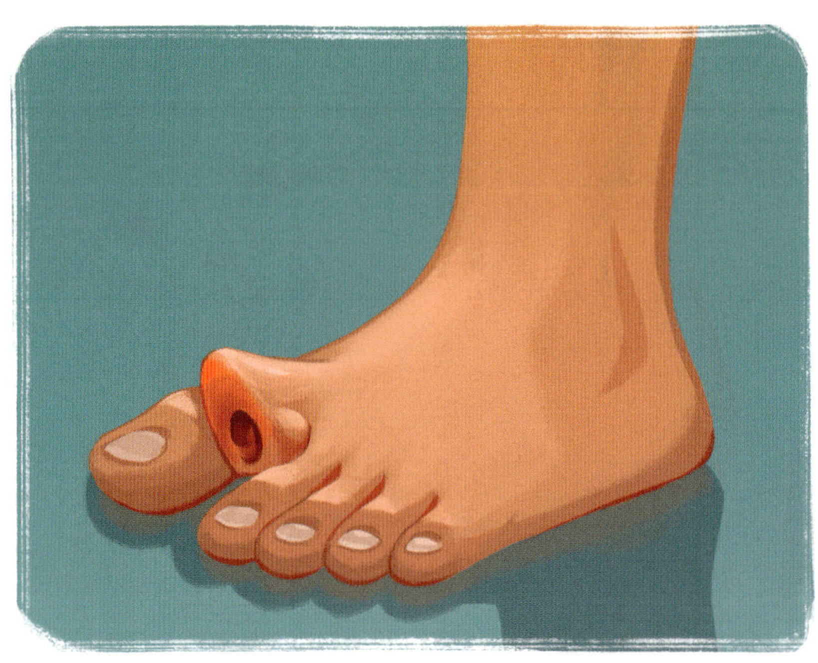

Your nose would be a source of dread
were it attached atop your head,
it soon would drive you to despair,
forever tickled by your hair.

Within your ear, your nose would be
an absolute catastrophe,
for when you were obliged to sneeze,
your brain would rattle from the breeze.

Your nose, instead, through thick and thin,
remains between your eyes and chin,
not pasted on some other place—
be glad your nose is on your face!

Jack Prelutsky

When the World Turned Upside Down

The day when the world
turned upside down:
when a frown became a smile
and a smile became a frown.

When the mice chased the cats
the cats chased the dogs.
The dogs laughed out loud
at the pink and yellow frogs.

When you went to bed in the daytime
and got up at night.
When birds caught the school bus
and the cows took flight.

When the moon came out
in the middle of the day
and all of the ocean's fish
rolled around in the hay.

When the children ruled the world
and ice cream was for free
and the elephants shrank
to the size of a flea.

When the grass rained lollipops
up to the sky.
When you wanted to laugh
but could only cry.

When magic beans were real
and giants very small,
you would eat spiders legs
so you could creep up the wall.

This all happened when the
world turned upside down
after I went to bed
with a smile – not a frown.

Margaret A. Savage

Five Eyes

In Hans' old Mill his three black cats
Watch the bins for the thieving rats.
Whisker and claw, they crouch in the night,
Their five eyes smouldering green and bright:
Squeaks from the flour sacks, squeaks from where
The cold wind stirs on the empty stair,
Squeaking and scampering, everywhere.
Then down they pounce, now in, now out,
At whisking tail, and sniffing snout;
While lean old Hans he snores away
Till peep of light at break of day;
Then up he climbs to his creaking mill,
Out come his cats all grey with meal —
Jekkel, and Jessup, and one-eyed Jill.

Walter de la Mare

Message From Nature

The mountains tell me, hold your head high.
Whatever be the problem, look it in the eye.

The rivers tell me, don't look behind.
March on ahead, till your goal you find.

The sea tells me, have depth of character.
The waves call out, don't forget your laughter!

The trees tell me, do good to one and all.
Let go of the past, like I let my leaves fall.

The sun tells me, you must go on shining.
In every dark cloud, be the silver lining.

Have a look at nature, and you will see,
There's so much to learn, just like me!

Kshma Lal

The Dentist and the Crocodile

The crocodile, with cunning smile, sat in the dentist's chair.
He said, "Right here and everywhere my teeth require repair."
The dentist's face was turning white. He quivered, quaked and shook.
He muttered, "I suppose I'm going to have to take a look."
"I want you", Crocodile declared, "to do the back ones first.
The molars at the very back are easily the worst."
He opened wide his massive jaws. It was a fearsome sight –
At least three hundred pointed teeth, all sharp and shining white.
The dentist kept himself well clear. He stood two yards away.
He chose the longest probe he had to search out the decay.

"I said to do the *back ones* first!" the Crocodile called out.
"You're much too far away, dear sir, to see what you're about.
To do the back ones properly you've got to put your head
Deep down inside my great big mouth," the grinning Crocky said.
The poor old dentist wrung his hands and, weeping in despair,
He cried, "No no! I see them all extremely well from here!"
Just then, in burst a lady, in her hands a golden chain.
She cried, "Oh Croc, you naughty boy, you're playing tricks again!"
"Watch out!" the dentist shrieked and started climbing up the wall.
"He's after me! He's after you! He's going to eat us all!"
"Don't be a twit," the lady said, and flashed a gorgeous smile.
"He's harmless. He's my little pet, my lovely crocodile."

Roald Dahl

The Moon

The moon has a face like the clock in the hall;
She shines on thieves on the garden wall,
On streets and fields and harbour quays,
And birdies asleep in the forks of the trees.

The squalling cat and the squeaking mouse,
The howling dog by the door of the house,
The bat that lies in bed at noon,
All love to be out by the light of the moon.

But all of the things that belong to the day
Cuddle to sleep to be out of her way;
And flowers and children close their eyes
Till up in the morning the sun shall arise.

Robert Louis Stevenson

Snake

Suddenly the grass before my feet
shakes and becomes alive.
The Snake
twists, almost leaps
graceful even in terror,
smoothness looping back over smoothness,
slithers away, disappears.
And the grass is again still.

And surely, by whatever means of communication
is available to Snakes,
the word is passed:
Hey, I just met a man, a monster too;
must have been oh seven feet tall
So keep away from the long grass,
it's dangerous there.

Ian Mudie

The Pied Piper of Hamelin

This text is part of a longer poem.

Into the street the Piper stept,
Smiling first a little smile,
As if he knew what magic slept
In his quiet pipe the while;
Then, like a musical adept,
To blow the pipe his lips he wrinkled,
And green and blue his sharp eyes twinkled,
Like a candle-flame where salt is sprinkled;

And ere three shrill notes the pipe uttered,
You heard as if an army muttered;
And the muttering grew to a grumbling;
And the grumbling grew to a mighty rumbling;
And out of the houses the rats came tumbling.

Great rats, small rats, lean rats, brawny rats,
Brown rats, black rats, gray rats, tawny rats,
Grave old plodders, gay young friskers,
Fathers, mothers, uncles, cousins,
Cocking tails and pricking whiskers,
Families by tens and dozens,
Brothers, sisters, husbands, wives—
Followed the Piper for their lives.

From street to street he piped advancing,
And step for step they followed dancing,
Until they came to the river Weser
Wherein all plunged and perished!

Robert Browning